the music thief

the music thief

peni r. griffin

Henry Holt and Company - New York

Henry Holt and Company, LLC
Publishers since 1866
115 West 18th Street
New York, New York 10011
www.henryholt.com

Library of Congress Cataloging-in-Publication Data
Griffin, Peni R. The music thief / Peni R. Griffin
p.   cm.
Summary: Living in San Antonio, Texas, eleven-year-old Alma tries to cope with the
drive-by shooting death of her favorite Latina singer, as well as deal with the struggles
of her various family members, and finds herself doing something she knows is wrong.
[1. Conduct of life—Fiction. 2. Family problems—Fiction. 3. Family
life—Texas—Fiction. 4. Hispanic Americans—Fiction. 5. Music—Fiction.
6. Gangs—Fiction. 7. San Antonio (Tex.)—Fiction.] I. Title.
PZ7.G88136 Mu 2002   [Fic]—dc21   2002024089

ISBN 0-8050-7055-9 / First Edition—2002 / Designed by Donna Mark
Printed in the United States of America on acid-free paper. ∞
1   3   5   7   9   10   8   6   4   2

For Carmen "T" the mosquito and all the poderitos

—P. R. G.

the music thief

- 1 -

the *letter*

The day after school let out, Alma put the new Jovita tape into her player on low volume, so as not to wake her baby niece, and wrote a letter. She sat sideways at the changing table, the paper springy between her felt-tip pen and the vinyl cushion, while Silvita napped in the fluttery shadow of the curtains. Alma wrote with none of her usual frowning difficulty. Jovita wasn't a teacher. She would understand a letter that slid between English and Spanish in midsentence, like the ordinary speech of most people Alma knew. The only problem was to make Jovita feel the way Alma wanted her to feel.

Alma wrote her letter in Spanglish, but in English it would have said:

Dear Jovita,

You are the greatest singer in the world, and I am proud that you live in my town. Even though you live on the south side and I live closer to the middle, I am still proud because it is all San Antonio. I am listening to my tape of your new album, and it is the best album I have ever heard. Your other albums are good, too, but this is the best. I can't play your music loud because it would wake up my niece, Silvita. She lives in my room since my grandmother died. My grandmother would let me play your music as much as I wanted, but babies need sleep. Abuela and I would play your music real loud, and she wanted for us to play "La florita" at her funeral, but Mama said we shouldn't play dance music at a funeral. I don't know why not if it was what Abuela wanted. She liked the parts about the flowers coming back every year.

Someday I will be a singer like you and play instruments with a band and maybe be famous. Or maybe I will just play for people to dance to my songs. As long as I play music, that's the main thing. I can almost read music, they taught us the notes on a little recorder at school, but I know it is hard work and you have to have an instrument and practice a lot. My brother, Eddie, used to play saxophone in band and he practiced all the time and never sounded right. Lalo, my sister's husband, showed me some chords on his accordion, but he had to sell it when Silvita was born. Eddie says girls don't make good musicians, but you are proof he doesn't know what he's talking about. Lalo says if you work hard enough you can do what you want to do, and he's right, because you did. I am eleven and will start middle school in the fall. They don't teach accordion at middle school, but maybe I can learn guitar or something.

The title cut on your album is coming on and I wish I could turn it up, but Silvita is napping. All your songs are good, but "La luna de agosto" is the best one, and someday maybe I will hear you play it at a concert. I hope so.

Tu amiga,

Alma Perez

Alma chewed the pen's plastic cap and read this over. There was still a little room left at the bottom of the page. *P.S.,* she wrote, *School is over. This is not a school project. It's what I really truly feel in my heart and I wanted you to know.*

There! She was glad she'd put in the part about "in my heart," because *"En mi corazón"* had been her favorite song till Jovita's new album came out. She folded the paper neatly into thirds and went to the living room to find a stamp and an envelope.

Lalo was at the desk, copying his class notes, and Eddie slept on the couch. Alma hesitated, hovering behind her brother-in-law's chair. He didn't like to be disturbed while he was studying, but the mail would be here soon and she wanted to get the letter out today.

"What is it, Alma?" asked Lalo.

"I need a stamp and an envelope," she said. "I'm sorry."

Lalo opened the center drawer and passed them to her. "Writing to your boyfriend?"

Alma glanced over at Eddie. He *looked* asleep. "Jovita."

"That singer? Where you going to get her address?" Lalo leaned back in his chair and stretched.

"Out of the phone book," Alma said.

"A big star like her won't have a listed number. Better send it care of her record company."

"She'll be in the phone book, all right. Or anyway, her mama will be."

"But you don't know her mama's name."

"Do too. It's on the tape below the playlist. *A mi mamá, Lourdes Ramos de Aguilar.*" She pulled the battered white pages out from under the phone. "Here, I'll show you." Alma found her easily and held the page out to Lalo with her finger under the name. "See? And Jovita lives with her mother. I saw it on TV."

"Well, what do you know?" said Lalo. "If I was a big star, I sure wouldn't let everybody know where I was. And I wouldn't be living in that crummy part of town, either. I'd be out in the Dominion with the millionaires."

"But Jovita's not like that," Alma informed him proudly. "She's staying in the same neighborhood she grew up in, and fixing up her mama's house, and giving money to parks and community centers and things. 'Cause she's not all selfish and stuck-up like most rich people. She wants to make things better for her friends."

"Yeah, for her homeys," said Eddie, rolling over.

Alma glared at him. "Jovita doesn't have homeys!"

"Does too," said Eddie. "And you know it. It was on the same TV show. Your perfect Jovita is one of Las Howling Madres."

"She is not!" yelled Alma. "She left the gang ages and ages ago! You take that back right now!"

"People don't leave gangs, except in a box," said Eddie. "Gangs are your family."

"Only if you're a loser," Lalo replied. "Gangs're kid stuff. And speaking of loser kid stuff, where were you last night?"

"None of your business," growled Eddie. "You're not my brother."

"I am now," said Lalo.

Alma hurriedly copied Jovita's mother's address onto the envelope and took it out to stick on the mailbox with the fistful of bills Mama had paid last night. Lalo and Eddie's argument about gangs veered into an argument about Eddie getting a job. Next door, Mrs. B.'s smallest cat, the gray tiger, stalked something, and Mrs. B. herself weeded her flower bed, singing some Anglo song about where all the flowers had gone, which made sense, because the flower bed didn't have as many flowers in it as it had when Mr. B. was alive.

Alma shied away from the thought. Thinking about dead Mr. B. was almost like thinking about her dead grandmother, and she didn't want to.

It was bad enough that Silvita's crib took up the same corner of the room as Abuela's bed had; that the changing table replaced Abuela's rocking armchair. She didn't need to remember how she and Abuela used to sit out here in the evenings, eating *paletas* and listening to the radio or to Mrs. B. playing piano next door. *Paletas* were frozen fruit juice on a stick, and Alma never ate one faster than it could melt down her arms. Mr. B. would be working in his yard, and he would wave at them when he came out and again when he went back in. Eddie would play touch football in the street with the boys that used to live on the corner, using the oak trees between the sidewalks and the curbs as yard markers and goals. Rosalia would practice cheers with her friend Marisol. When the radio played a really good number, Abuela would teach the girls and Eddie the *baile,* kicking off her flip-flops to dance barefoot on the dusty drive.

The long twilights were perfect and whole in Alma's head. No matter how hard she tried, she could not shut her brain down fast enough to keep herself from remembering all of them and feeling the stab in her chest that was the knowledge there wouldn't be any more.

Way in the back of the house, Silvita started crying. Mama and Rosalia were at their weekend jobs; Lalo needed to finish his note copying and get ready for his weekend job. Eddie always acted as if Silvita didn't exist. Alma hurried inside, thinking how pleased Jovita would be to get her letter.